Scarecrow

WRITTEN BY

Cynthia Rylant

ILLUSTRATED BY

Lauren Stringer

Harcourt Brace & Company

San Diego   New York   London

Rylant, Cynthia.
Scarecrow/Cynthia Rylant; illustrated by Lauren Stringer.
p.   cm.
Summary: Although made of straw and borrowed clothes,
a scarecrow appreciates his peaceful, gentle life
and the privilege of watching nature at work.
ISBN 0-15-201084-X
[1. Scarecrows—Fiction.] I. Stringer, Lauren, ill. II. Title.
PZ7.R982Sc 1998
[E]—dc20 96-7652

First edition
A C E F D B
Printed in Singapore

The illustrations in this book were done in
Lascaux acrylics on Arches 150-lb. watercolor paper.
The display type was set in OptiMarcus.
The text type was set in Minister Light.
Color separations by Bright Arts, Ltd., Singapore
Printed and bound by Tien Wah Press, Singapore
This book was printed on totally chlorine-free
Nymolla Matte Art paper.
Production supervision by Stanley Redfern
Designed by Lauren Stringer and Lydia D'moch

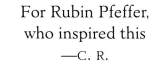

For Rubin Pfeffer,
who inspired this
—C. R.

For Matthew,
who fills my life with colors
I can see and hear
—L. S.

His hat is borrowed, his suit is borrowed, his hands are borrowed, even his head is borrowed. And his eyes probably came out of someone's drawer.

But a scarecrow's life is all his own.

It takes a certain peace, hanging around a garden all day. It takes a love of silence and air. A liking for long, slow thoughts. A friendliness toward birds.

Yes, birds. Crows, grackles, starlings, jays. Ask them how they feel about a scarecrow, and they'll say, "Lovely." They ignore the pie-pan hands and the button eyes and see instead the scarecrow's best gift: his gentleness.

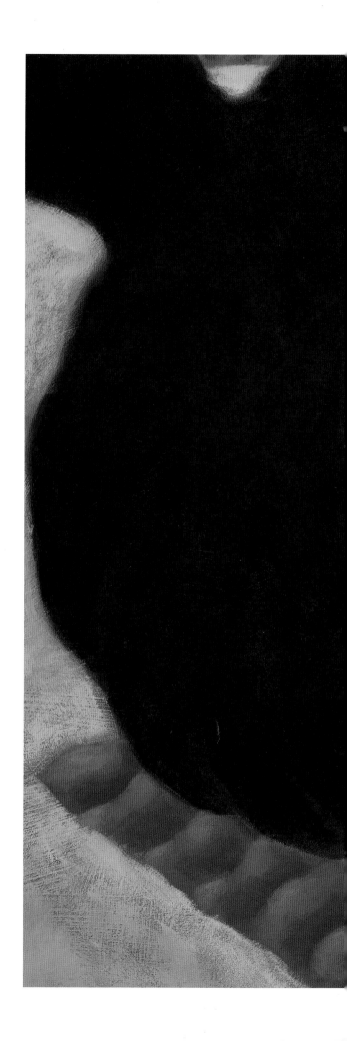

They line up on his arms
and can chat all day.

He knows he isn't real. A scarecrow understands right away that he is just borrowed parts made to look like somebody.

But he knows this, too: that there is a certain wonder going on around him. Seeds are being planted, and inside them there are ten-foot-tall sunflowers and mammoth pumpkins and beans that just go on forever.

And though the scarecrow
knows that he can as quickly
be turned back into straw
and buttons as he was turned
into a man, he doesn't care.

He has been with the
owls in evening and the
rabbits at dawn. He has
watched a spider work
for hours making a web
like lace. He has seen
the sun tremble and the
moon lie still.

The scarecrow doesn't care what he is made of or how long he might last, for he has been a witness to life. The earth has rained and snowed and blossomed and wilted and yellowed and greened and vined itself all around him.

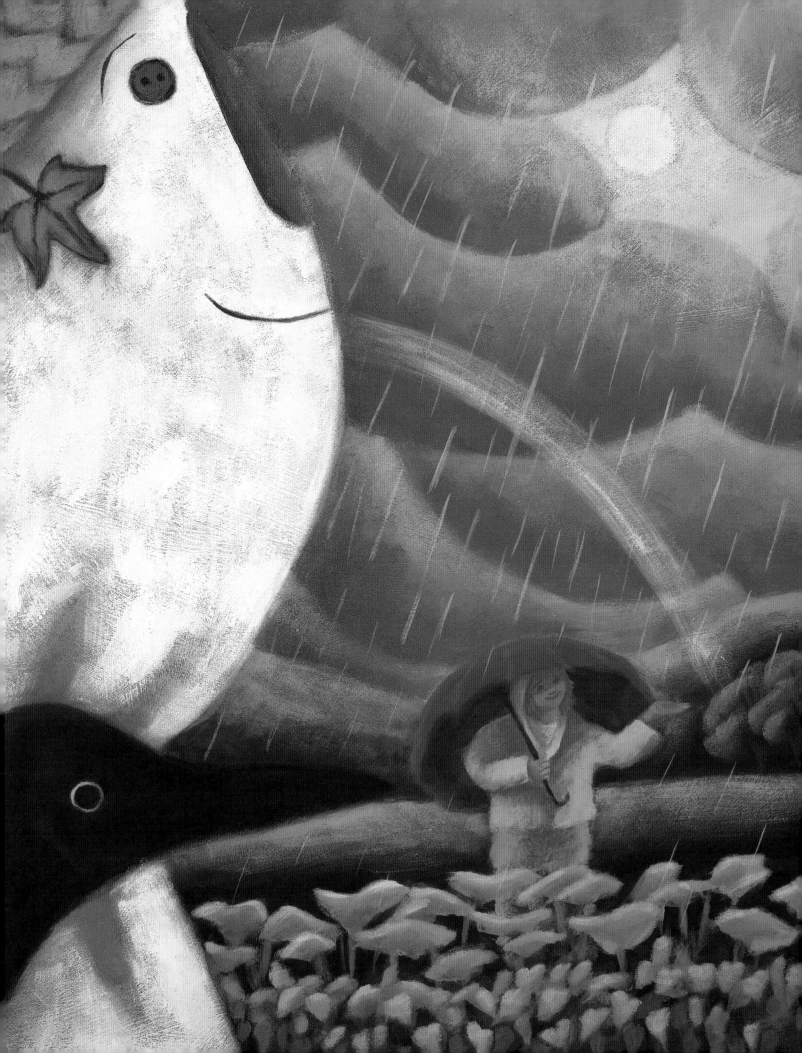

His hat has housed mice and
his arms have rested birds.
A morning glory has held tight
to his legs and a worm is living
in his lapel.

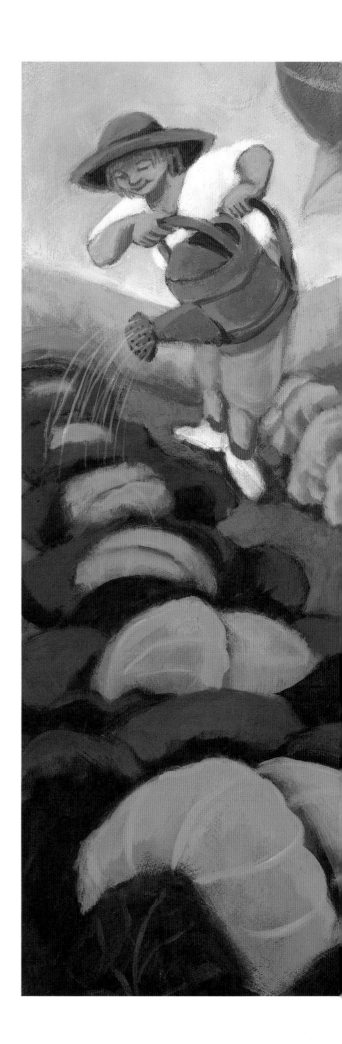

There is not much else a person might want, and the scarecrow knows this.

So he doesn't mind that there is always a smile on his face or that his eyes are always open. He doesn't mind being up high. He doesn't mind staying there.

The wind is brushing his borrowed head
and the sun is warming his borrowed hands
and clouds are floating across his
button-borrowed eyes.

The scarecrow is thinking his
long, slow thoughts . . .

. . . and soon, birds will
be coming by.